FRIZZ

Ellen Frances

Illustrated by Coral Tulloch

SupaDoopers

sundance
A Haights Cross Communications Company

Published by
Sundance Publishing
P.O. Box 1326
234 Taylor Street
Littleton, MA 01460
800-343-8204
www.sundancepub.com

First published 1999 by
Addison Wesley Longman Australia Pty Limited
95 Coventry Street
South Melbourne 3205 Australia
Exclusive United States Distribution: Sundance Publishing

ISBN 0-7608-6635-X

Printed in Canada

Contents

Chapter 1

Big Trouble

t was the worst moment of Kim's life! She'd been practicing for tomorrow night's ballet recital for weeks.

But at the dress rehearsal, everything had gone wrong. Mom couldn't get Kim's long straight hair to stay in place. And then the sash on her costume was too long.

And later, as Kim danced across the stage, several bobby pins fell out. Her long black locks flopped over her eyes.

Poor Kim! She tripped on her sash and stumbled into the prince and princess, and all three of them fell into the fountain!

Kim sat up and flipped the hair from her face. Everyone was laughing at her. Prince Lucas was smiling as he helped Princess Holly stand up. She stomped over to Kim. "You're a real clown!" she exploded. Then she rushed into the arms of her fussing mother.

Lucas dusted himself off as he walked past Kim. "Are you OK?" he asked her. Kim smiled at him from the floor. Holly ran back and dragged him away to do some more practice.

Kim's mother came to help her daughter stand up. She shook her head thoughtfully. Then she said, "I think the problem is that your hair's too straight. Aunt Zenda's coming over tonight to color my hair. I'll give her a call and see if she can perm your hair. Then you'll have lots of little curls that will help your bobby pins stay in."

Kim started feeling better. Aunt Zenda was really good at fixing hair. Everyone said that she should have been a hairdresser.

Chapter 2

Aunt Zenda
to the Rescue

That evening, as Aunt Zenda rolled Kim's hair onto curlers, Kim told her what had happened.

"Don't you worry, dear," Aunt Zenda gushed. "When I've finished, you'll be so lovely that Lucas will want to be dancing with you, instead of that horrible Holly."

Kim could hear her twin brothers arguing in their bedroom. "They're mine!" yelled Michael. "They're not!" shouted Bernard. "They're mine, mine, mine!"

Kim watched Aunt Zenda mix Mom's hair dye in a basin next to the sink.

Then her aunt said, "OK, Kim, let's do your perm first." She led Kim to the sink and began pouring the perming solution over the rollers in Kim's hair.

"Give it to me!" screamed Michael.

"Make me!" yelled Bernard, as the two boys burst from their room and raced through the kitchen.

"Look out!" shouted Mom.

Bernard ducked behind Aunt Zenda just as
Michael ran into her. Poor Aunt Zenda
was knocked sideways, and perming
solution poured all over Kim's hair.

And as Aunt Zenda lurched to the side, Kim tumbled headfirst into the basin of hair dye!

Mom yelled at the boys. Aunt Zenda helped Kim remove her head from the basin. She quickly poured something else over Kim's hair, rinsed it, and dried it off.

"Oh my!" said Aunt Zenda.

"Oh dear!" groaned Mom. She handed Kim a mirror.

Kim screamed.

Chapter 3

The Family Digs In

Mom sent the twins to school early the next morning. She said if they told anyone about Kim's hair, she'd never cook for them again. The boys believed her.

"As if I wouldn't!" Mom whispered to Grandma. Grandma had hurried over as soon as Aunt Zenda had phoned. Grandma gave Kim a hug. "It's a pretty shade of green," she said.

Kim tried to smile.

"Aunt Zenda and I are going to the Hair Central store today. We'll find something to help."

Later in the morning, they sped off on Grandma's motorcycle.

Uncle Elliot arrived. He was surprised to see how bright Kim's hair was. "Don't you worry," he told her. "I've brought some of my compost tea. It's been brewing for four weeks and should be strong enough to fix anything."

He took Kim outside and made her bend over the roses. Very carefully, he poured the brown liquid over her hair.

"It stinks!" wailed Kim.

Uncle Elliot winked at her. "It kills insects as well!" he crowed.

But when he washed the mixture off,
Kim's hair was still as green as ever.

"And now it stinks!" howled Kim.

Grandma and Aunt Zenda roared up the driveway on the motorcycle.

R-o-a-r-r-r-r-r-r-r

"What are you up to?" Grandma asked
Uncle Elliot. She sniffed Kim's hair. "Not
your compost tea!" Shaking her head in
disbelief, she took Kim back inside.

Aunt Zenda pulled some bottles from a bag. As Kim bent over the sink, Aunt Zenda drained the contents of the large bottle over her hair. Then she did the same with the smaller one.

When she was done, Aunt Zenda rinsed Kim's hair well. Then she said, "Stand up, Kim. Let's have a look."

Kim stood up. Purple drips ran down her neck and onto her nose.

"Oh my!" said Aunt Zenda.

"Interesting!" said Grandma.

"Oh dear!" sighed Mom, and she passed the mirror to Kim.

Kim screamed. Now her hair had *purple streaks* running along the green, frizzy strands!

Chapter 4

It's Getting Late

Nobody spoke while they ate lunch. They were all trying to think of what to do about Kim's hair.

After lunch, Mom measured and shortene[d]
the sash that went on Kim's costume.

Kim went to her room. She dragged on red tights, tied on red ballet slippers, and slipped into her red costume.

She looked in the mirror and screamed.

In the other room, Mom and Grandma exchanged worried glances.

"I look like a tomato!" she wailed.

She was right!

Just then, Kim heard a tap on her bedroom window. It was her cousin Zac.

"I heard about your problem," he said. He handed her a bottle of vinegar. "It stripped the paint off my car," he explained.

Changing out of her costume and into some old clothes, Kim climbed through the window. She washed her hair in the vinegar and rinsed it off in the birdbath.

Kim stood up, shaking water from her ears.

"Hey, cool!" admired Zac.

Kim looked at herself in the side-view mirror on Zac's car. Now her hair had purple *and* white streaks, mixed in with the green frizz! But that gave her an idea!

Chapter 5

Kim's Fashion Statement

That night, Grandma, Aunt Zenda, Uncle Elliot, and Mom were very worried. When they went to get Kim, she couldn't be found. But then cousin Zac phoned to say that he knew where she was, and he would bring her to the recital.

The twins were pushing and pulling each other as the family found their seats in the theater.

"Do you think she's all right?" Mom asked Grandma as the lights dimmed and the recital began.

Grandma patted Mom's arm.

The prince and princess swirled across the stage. Their servants danced in a line behind them.

"I don't see her," whispered a worried Aunt Zenda.

But suddenly, there she was! Kim twirled across the stage and flashed a smile at Lucas. "Cool!" he whispered, as she leaped past him. Holly looked furious!

Kim flicked her hair and danced into line. The many colorful plaits that she and Zac had braided that afternoon jiggled. When the audience saw Kim's "dancing hair," they clapped and cheered. They loved it!

When Kim talked to a newspaper reporter after the recital, she explained, "I wanted to make a fashion statement." And she beamed at Lucas as he came toward her.

Lucas lifted her hand to his lips and kissed it. "You're a real star!" he said.

And Kim could only agree!

About the Author

Ellen Frances

Ellen Frances likes to believe there are stories hiding everywhere, waiting to be discovered.

Originally from Melbourne, Australia, Ellen has taught school, from the elementary grades through high school.

Ellen has also worked as a jazz singer, storyteller, children's TV columnist, scriptwriter, journalist, photographer, and author.

Ellen now lives in the United States and continues to explore new and different ways to tell a good story.

About the Illustrator

Coral Tulloch (that's me) lives on an island that has snow on the mountain in winter,.... And with her daughter Tully, her husband Peter and step-daughter Isabella,.... And with a [porcupine] Called Pea who likes to eat parsley... And a [dog] Called RED, who likes to eat boiled [egg]s & who you Can See on the [island] above.

Tully likes to eat her [egg]s with faces drawn on them. Isabella likes chocolate ones. Coral likes spinach & Peter likes [fish] which is a good thing if you live in a street like ours with a pier at the end!